The
VEGETARIAN
WEREWOLF

THE VEGETARIAN WEREWOLF

COLIN FLETCHER

Illustrated by
Leonard O'Grady

POOLBEG
FOR CHILDREN

Published 2002
by Poolbeg Press Ltd
123 Grange Hill, Baldoyle
Dublin 13, Ireland
E-mail: poolbeg@poolbeg.com

© Colin Fletcher 2002

Copyright for typesetting, layout, design
© Poolbeg Group Services Ltd.

The moral right of the author has been asserted.

1 3 5 7 9 10 8 6 4 2

A catalogue record for this book is available from the British Library.

ISBN 1 84223 021 2

Cover design by Steven Hope
Illustrations by Leonard O'Grady
Typeset by Patricia Hope in Times 16/24
Printed by
The Guernsey Press Ltd,
Vale, Guernsey, Channel Islands.

www.poolbeg.com

About the Author

Colin Fletcher left school when he was fifteen and worked for nine years as an electrician in East Suffolk. When he was twenty-four he moved to Norwich where he trained as a teacher. He taught for twenty-three years in primary and middle schools in Suffolk and Norfolk. He has now left full-time teaching and spends most of his working week writing for children. He lives alone on the Suffolk coast and has two grown-up daughters. His other books include *The Worst Class In The School* and *The Wishing Race*, also published by Poolbeg.

For the children of Coldfair Green Primary School
who helped me with this story

"You're too small to play football!" Tom's mother told him.

"I'M NOT! I'M NOT!" he shouted.

"Yes, you are!" she said. "You'd get knocked over and hurt, darling."

"I WOULDN'T! I WOULDN'T!" he yelled. "I'm really tough!" And he skidded across his bedroom and squashed a pillow against his wardrobe with a fantastic sliding tackle.

"It's no good," she said. "You are *not*

1

going to football practice tomorrow morning!"

"But everyone goes!" Tom protested.

"Yes, but they're bigger than you, sweetheart."

"But I'm as old as them! I'm a Year Three, same as they are!"

"I know but you're only a very tiny Year Three, Tom, aren't you? You're even smaller than the Year Ones, darling."

"I'm not!"

"You're Mummy's Tiny Tom, you are! And she has to look after you, sweetie."

"Don't call me sweetie!" Why did everyone treat him like a baby? Just because he was a bit little! "Short people can be good at footie, you know!" he said, dodging and swerving like Michael Owen. "I'm brilliant at dribbling. Look!"

"No, Tom. You're not going. You can come into town with Daddy and me."

Oh no! Not the dreaded shopping torture again!

"And on the way back we can go to Toddlers' Tumble Land!"

"BUT I'M NOT A TODDLER! I'M SEVEN! NEARLY EIGHT!"

"You know how you like Tumble Land!"

"I DON'T!"

"And you can take Teddy. Teddy likes Tumble Land too, don't you, Teddy?"

"TUMBLE LAND IS STUPID!" Tom bellowed. "TEDDY IS STUPID! EVERYTHING IS STUPID!"

"Temper, temper!" his mother

scolded. "I'm going downstairs now, anyway. Nighty-night." And out she went. "And you'd better get some sleep!" she called back. "We want an early start in the morning."

Tom was so angry he just *threw* the stupid teddy down and jump-tackled it! Then he spun brilliantly and kicked it hard across his bedroom – one of his perfect, curving banana-shots – right into the top corner of his door where Jamie, the school goalie would *never* reach it! "GOAL! TOM SCORES AGAIN!" he shouted. Then he dribbled superbly round his chair, pretending it was Briggsy, the school captain. He zigzagged past him like Ryan Giggs, leaned over and volleyed another fantastic shot – WHAM! – into the net!

If only Mr Bunn could see him shoot like

that! If only they could *all* see! Then they'd *definitely* put him in the team on Tuesday, for the great Schools' Cup Final! But how could they? They never even let him play at school! Not even at breaktimes! They said he was *too little*! And *too weedy*! Well, he *wasn't*! He was *speedy*! And *tricky*! And *a super shooter*! "EVEN IF I'M LITTLE," he yelled, "I CAN STILL PLAY FOOTIE!"

* * *

Did you know that if a werewolf creeps past your house it makes the lights flicker? It does. And if it comes real close – like up to your window – they go out completely!

Tom was playing *Tackle the Teddy* when his light began to *blink*. He looked up . . . and it went right out . . . and left him in blackness! Then a branch began scratching on his window. *But there weren't any branches out there!* What could it be?

He felt his way along his bed . . . over to the window . . . and . . . YANKED the curtains back!

A *WEREWOLF*! A *real* one!

"Coo! Fantastic!"

It was HUGE!

"Great!"

And its mouth was all blood-red!

"Cool!" Tom wished *he* was huge and *his* mouth was all blood-red!

Now, Tom's parents had never told him what to do if a werewolf appeared at his window. So he just did what he thought was polite. "Hold on a minute," he told it. "I'll let you in." He pushed the window open and stood back . . . and the hairy beast squeezed through.

Tom didn't know that werewolves bite your neck and pierce your arteries with their fangs and suck your blood. So he just shook hands as he'd been taught to do when meeting a guest. "Pleased to meet you," he said.

7

"Oh, pleased to eat *you*!" the werewolf growled, as *he'd* been taught to do if ever he met a soft and yummy-looking child.

Tom wondered why his new friend pounced at him with his tongue flapping and his eyes rolling. He thought it must be some kind of special werewolfy greeting . . .

Tom never felt the fangs biting his neck.

And he never felt the lips gulping his blood.

Because the werewolf just *cuddled* him! And began to cry like a baby. "I hate being a werewolf! I hate it!" he sobbed.

Tom's light flashed on again. "Coo! You must be mad!" he said. "I'd love to be a great big werewolf, I would!"

The werewolf pulled out a pretty lace handkerchief. "It's horrible!" he blubbered. "Disgusting! The way we have to go round sucking people's blood! I'd just *love* to be tiny and sweet and gentle, like you!"

"I'M NOT TINY AND SWEET AND

GENTLE! I'M SPEEDY! AND TRICKY!
AND A SUPER SHOOTER!" Tom yelled,
tackling it hard.

"Don't hit me!" the werewolf whimpered.
"I've had such a difficult week! My
girlfriend has kicked me out! Just because
I won't touch her revolting blood-burgers!

Or that horrible
blood-cola! She
knows I can't stand
the sight of blood!"
Some werewolf!

"But, talking of
food," he said,
staring dreamily at Tom's supper tray, "is that
really a bottle of tomato sauce?" He didn't
wait for an answer. He just leapt across the
room, stabbed his fangs into the plastic bottle
and sucked it empty with one great slurp!

What a hoover-mouth!

"Aah!" he sighed. "I just love tomatoes! Tomato doughnuts! Tomato custard! Tomato ice cream! I dream about 'em!" Then Wolfie made a big decision. "I'm never touching blood again!" he announced. "From now on I'm A NO-SUCKING ZONE!"

"You know what you are?" Tom realised. "You're a vegetarian, that's what you are. A vegetarian werewolf!"

"Oh!" he said, proudly. "I'm a vegetarian! Do you hear that?" He skipped a little dance and started to sing:

"I'm a vegetarian!

I'm not a vege-scare-ian!

Don't care if folks all stare-ian!

'Cos I'm a vege-rare-ian!"

Tom had this *brilliant* idea – *Plan*

Number One. "Hey, Wolfie! Stand still! Stand still!" he shouted, pushing him onto his bed. "Why don't we *change places*?"

"Change places?"

"Yeah! You could be me and I could be you!"

"What, I could live here? And pretend to be *a little boy*?"

"Yeah! Then you could go to Toddlers' Tumble Land." *Plan Number Two!*

"Oh, Toddlers' Tumble Land!" Wolfie said, clapping his hands. "How delightful!"

That should teach them a lesson! "And on Monday, you can come to school and play with the other boys." *Plan Number Three!* Tom grinned at the thought of the boys trying to tell a *werewolf* that he was too weedy to play football.

"How charming! Playing with little boys!" Wolfie said dreamily.

"And you gotta ask them if I can be in the school team." *Plan Number Four!*

"Oh, I'm sure they'll let you."

"Yeah! I reckon they will!" Tom agreed. "Then, at midnight, Wolfie, *you* can take *me* werewolfing! Deal?"

"Deal!" Wolfie said.

"Right! You get in my bed then. Okay?"

It was really hard trying to force

Wolfie's huge hairy legs into Tom's pyjama bottoms. "When my mum brings up my tomato juice in the morning," Tom said, tucking him in, "you just give her one of your big, wolfy smiles, okay?" *Plan Number Five!*

"Oh, tomato juice!" Wolfie sang, gripping

the quilt. "How exciting! I'll never be able to sleep!"

* * *

Next morning, Tom watched from his spy-hole under the bed as his mother came in with his tray.

"Tomsy-womsy! Wakey-uppy!" she sang at the lump in the bed. She held out a bunch of pansies and the lump sighed happily. "Mummy has a surprise-y for her beautiful little boy-y!" she trilled.

"And her beautiful little boy-y has a surprise-y for her-er!" Tom thought.

She closed her eyes, pulled back the quilt and bent to kiss her sweet little angel.

"Oh, she wants to kiss me!" Wolfie thought. "How lovely!" And he pushed his cold, wet mouth onto hers.

The whole of Primrose Avenue heard "YEE-EE-EE-EE-EE-EEK!". Tom saw the flowers flying everywhere. And his mother rolled over backwards with her legs in the air.

"Oh, kiss me! Kiss me!" Wolfie pleaded gruffly.

But she just scrambled out of the room

and fled downstairs, yelling "Albert! Albert! Tom's not Tom any more! He's grown HUGE! While he was asleep!"

Wolfie began bawling and stamping. "This *always* happens! *Always!*" he sobbed. "Whenever I try to be nice!"

"Now she knows what I'm *really* like!" Tom sniggered.

* * *

Sarah-Jane, the play-leader, had never seen a little boy like Wolfie at Toddlers' Tumble Land before. He was huge! His clothes were far too small and clumps of brown hair were sticking out all over the place. And his face was sort of . . . *like a wolf's*!

"Are you sure you're only four years old?" she asked him.

"Oh yes. And aren't I sweet?" Wolfie replied, fluttering his eyelashes. "Now, I simply *must* have a go on that seesaw."

Tom watched from behind the door as Wolfie padded over on all fours and grinned a wolfy grin at sweeet little Rosie. She took one look at his sparkling fangs and screamed, "Wa-a-ah! Mu-u-ummy!"

"Oh, look what he's done to poor Rosie!" Sarah-Jane yelled.

So Wolfie leapt a massive wolf-leap onto the Jack-and-the-beanstalk climbing frame . . . and completely flattened it!

"Oh, no!" Sarah-Jane moaned.

"Sorry-y-y!" he called over to them. Then he rolled right across the bouncy castle . . . accidentally squashing a few tiny tots. "Oh, let me rub it better," he told them, but his thorny claws spiked the castle

and it burst with a great WHOOSH! of air.
"Didn't mean it!" he wailed.

"HE'S RUINED EVERYTHING!" Sarah-
Jane yelled at Tom's mother. "YOUR
BOY'S MUCH TOO BIG FOR TUMBLE
LAND, YOU SILLY WOMAN!"

Tom's poor mother almost cried but he

just grinned. Things were turning out very well.

* * *

On Monday, Tom took Wolfie to school . . . and hid him in the PE shed. "See you at breaktime," he whispered.

"Ooh!" Wolfie trilled, clapping his hands. "Then I can play with the dear little children."

* * *

The Cup Final team had been pinned up in the library corner and the eleven players and two subs were slapping each other on the back. Tom couldn't get near it! They just kept ruffling his hair and pushing him back. *Just you wait till breaktime!* he thought.

21

When break came they were allowed on the field. "It's the team versus everyone else!" Briggsy bossed. But when Tom ran to the 'everyone else' end they just shouted "NOT YOU, TOM! YOU'RE TOO LITTLE!"

"I'm not!" he yelled. "I'm *speedy*! And *tricky*! And *a super shooter*!"

They just laughed and pushed him away. But Tom grabbed the ball and raced off . . . towards the PE shed!

"Put it down, *you little midget*," Briggsy yelled, chasing him, "or I'll *bash* you!"

Tom may have been small but he was also very fast and he easily got to the shed first.

"Quick!" he ordered Wolfie, stretching his school shirt over the werewolf's shoulders and cramming his baseball cap over his big ears. "NOW GO, WOLFIE! GO!"

When Briggsy saw the shed door opening he shouted, "I'm really gonna *thump* you, *Tom Thumb*!" But Tom looked different . . . sort of *bigger* . . . and kinda covered in . . . *hair*! And his mouth was *huge* and . . . and . . . *LIKE A WOLF'S*! "Mum-my! Gran-ma-aa! Auntie Violet!" he cried, running back towards the others.

"Wait for me-ee-ee!" Wolfie called. But what the boys heard was a bloodcurdling "WAI-EE-EE-EE!". He kicked the ball a great WALLOPING kick that sent it flying over the school roof! The terrified footballers just stared at him for one second, then they ran for the school door and piled up in a heap of bodies.

Wolfie pounced on poor Briggsy and

tossed him high into the air as a kind of happy, wolfy hello. Then, as a sign of *real* wolfy friendship, he pushed his wet, bad-breath muzzle right into the boy's face. "Are you my friend?" he growled.

"S-sure!" Briggsy agreed. "Y-you can play f-footie any time you want to, T-Tom."

Wolfie had spotted a little ring of girls making daisy-chains. They looked *so sweet* and football was much too rough. So he left his new friend and crept up on them *as a little surprise*! "It's me-ee-ee!" he sang out. But they only heard "EE! EE—EE-EE!" and a wolf in a school uniform jumped at them!

"HELP!" they yelled, throwing six packets of tangy tomato crisps into the air.

"Ooh! Ta very much!" Wolfie said, wolfing them down, packets and all.

The girls ran off screaming and scrambled up the hill of boys.

"Oh, nobody likes me! Nobody!" Wolfie wailed. And he raced right back to the shed where he sat and vampired twenty-six rugby balls.

* * *

Back in the classroom Briggsy said, "C-come on, T-Tom. C-come and s-sit with us."

Tom went to shake hands but they just yelled and dived under the tables! Then Mr Bunn came in, waddling like a jelly and carrying a plateful of doughnuts – a little treat to last him till lunchtime.

"We want Tom in the team now," Briggsy said. "He can be third sub."

But Mr Bunn just laughed, splashing his bubbly hot chocolate over his hand. "You must be joking!" he spluttered. "Our Tiny Tom Thumb can't play footie. He's much too small for that! He can stand on the line and watch. That's the place for Tiny Tom Thumbs!"

"Just you wait, *Currant Bunn*!" Tom thought. "I'll get you for that!" *Plan Number Six!*

* * *

When Tom got home from school he had a big surprise! They'd papered his room with Premier League wallpaper! *"Excellent!"* And he'd got new Ipswich Town curtains! *"Wow!"* And a World Cup quilt! *"Cool!"*

"Look in your wardrobe, Tom," his dad told him.

And there . . . right in front of him . . . was . . . A BRAND NEW BLUE-AND-WHITE FOOTBALL STRIP! AND DAVID B E C K H A M BOOTS! *"Yes!"*

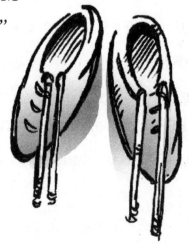

"Like it, Tom?"

"It's brilliant!" Tom fizzed. "Double brilliant! *Treble* brilliant!"

His mother just sighed. "Ah, well," she said. "I suppose you had to grow up sometime."

* * *

When they'd gone, Wolfie dragged himself out from under the bed. "I'm so depressed," he moaned, scoffing a tomato-and-tomato-sauce sandwich. "Nobody likes me. Just because I've got *fangs* and I'm covered in *hair* they think I'm a *werewolf*!"

"You *are* a werewolf," Tom told him.

"No-o!" he wailed, putting his paws over his ears.

"Well, you look like one, anyway!"

"Not listening!" he sobbed, curling up in a ball.

"Wolfie! Wolfie! It's almost dark!" Tom whispered. "And there's a super moon. Just right for werewolfing!"

"Can't hear you!" he called, pulling a pillow over his head.

"But you *promised*!" Tom reminded him. "We shook paws, remember?"

"Oh, I'm *always* being bullied! *Always!*" Wolfie complained, lifting Tom onto his back.

They leapt through the window . . . sprang over the garden fence . . . and bounded up the road. There was *someone* Tom very much wanted to visit. "That big house, there! Next to the garden centre," he pointed.

* * *

Mr Bunn had his enormous old shorts and his out-of-shape vest on. He was going to try those exercises again – well, after he'd just had these four little burgers . . . with onions . . . and tomato sauce . . . for energy. He took a squelchy bite . . . and his lights flickered. His tongue curled round a slippery tail of onion . . . and the lights went right out! "Oh dear. I'll have to open the curtains," he munched. "Let a little moonlight in."

When Tom saw the curtains opening he pulled his lips back and made his hairy scary face.

"Aah!" the fat teacher gasped, falling backwards. "It's T-TOM TH-THUMB! W-with a w-wolf's b-body!"

They leapt right on top of him. "P-PLEASE! S-SAVE ME!" he pleaded. "You can be in the team, T-Tom! P-promise!"

When the lights came on Wolfie spotted a splodge of ketchup on the fat cheek. "How-oo-oo-oo!" he howled, licking the whole face clean with his salivary, rough tongue.

Poor Mr Bunn just fainted and his head sploshed back into a bowl of custard he was saving for later.

"Now look what we've done!" Wolfie groaned. "I hate werewolfing! It's the worst way of eating out in the whole world!"

"Oh, come on then, you big baby," Tom agreed. "I'll take you to the garden centre and you can have a tomato! That'll cheer you up."

* * *

Wolfie smiled again when he saw the bulging tomatoes. "What whoppers!" he drooled, imagining the sweet juices bursting down his cheeks.

"Ssh!" Tom warned him. "There's someone coming!"

"Oh, look at *her*!" Wolfie gasped. Just up ahead of them, with a shopping basket over her arm, was *a girl werewolf*! "What a delicious dolly!" he said dreamily.

Even Tom could see she was pretty. She had blonde dyed fur, bright red claw-varnish and high-heeled back-paws. And she was humming her favourite love song.

Wolfie's face had gone all sort of soppy and he whistled a wild wolf whistle.

She trotted towards them in her high heels.

"Y-you w-won't h-hurt me, w-will you?" Tom muttered.

She put a paw on his head. "Why, what a

sweet little human-cub," she purred. "Hurt you, dearie? Wouldn't dream of it. Haven't touched a human-steak in years! Strictly vegetarian, me! *Tara the Tomataholic!*"

Wolfie's grin was almost splitting his head open now! "Allow me to offer you a seat," he begged.

"Why, what wonderful manners," she chirped. "You very rarely find good manners in a werewolf!"

The two of them sat chatting for ages. *He* offered *her* a "Cherry Red". *She* begged *him* to try a "Rose Round".

"And it's *so* old-fashioned to live in graveyards, these days," the Modern Miss Werewolf told him.

"Oh, I quite agree," Wolfie quite agreed. "When *I* get married, Tara, I'll dig myself a new semi-detached den in a decent neighbourhood."

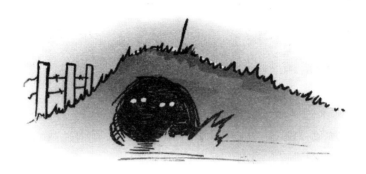

"Oh, yes!" she enthused. "In a posh forest!"

"With a garden! And a greenhouse, I mean *redhouse,*" he dreamed.

"And some of those lovely new *lair chairs*!" she said, grabbing his arm.

Tom was fed up. Wolfie had completely forgotten about *him.* "Come on, Wolfie!" he moaned. "We gotta get back."

* * *

As they bounded home, Wolfie sang dreamily:

"I'm in love,

I'm in love,

Tell the world

I'm in love!"

He back-flipped right over a house and looped-the-loop over a TV aerial.

"Slow down!" Tom grumped. "You've got a passenger, remember?"

* * *

Next morning, Tom went straight to the library corner. Mr Bunn jumped out of his way. "I've p-put you in, T-Tom," he quivered.

Tom read his name proudly. "Third sub! Yes!"

* * *

After school he ran home and put his kit on in front of the mirror. "But what about if I'm no good?" he asked Wolfie. "What about if I just *look* like a footballer?"

But Wolfie wasn't listening. He was almost crying. "She's the most wonderful creature in the whole wide world," he moaned.

"I mean, I've only played up here, kicking my socks and pants around."

"She could never love *me*? I mean, *who* could ever love *me*? I'm not even a proper werewolf, am I?"

"I might be *useless* with a real ball and real boys."

"I know what I'll do!" Wolfie said, jumping up. "I'll tell her! I'll say, *I think you're really nice, Tara! So let's GET MARRIED!*"

"And *everyone* will be watching! Dad. Mum. *Everyone!*"

"I'm off on a Tara hunt! SEE YER!"

"And they'll all think I'm weedy again! If I can't play."

Wolfie crashed through the window at a hundred miles an hour . . . and Tom dragged himself downstairs to put his boots on.

* * *

The whole school had come to see the game. And loads of parents. They'd never been in the final before.

Tom watched and waited with a coat on over his kit.

At half-time they were winning, one-nil. "I'm not changing a winning team," Mr Bunn announced, trying to sound like the England manager.

In the second half, Tom watched every kick. Sometimes his foot stabbed forward as if he was actually out there playing. He kept looking at Mr Bunn. He'd *never* get a game! Then . . . *they* scored! One-one. And only five minutes left!

"Numbers three, six and eight *off*! Subs *on*!" Mr Bunn screamed.

Tom threw his coat down and ran out onto the pitch. It looked *massive* and he

really did feel small now. Everyone was looking at him. He was *terrified*. And his tummy was all fluttery, like when he was going to be sick.

When the ball skidded towards him, Tom just yelped and jumped out of the way. Everyone laughed. "Come on!" he told himself. He ran and prodded the ball . . . and he was very surprised when it stuck to his boot like a magnet. Then he dragged it back with his other foot and it rolled perfectly for him. *Yes! He could do it!* He *could* play with a real ball! So he did what he always did in his bedroom. He whizzed off towards the goal. He zigzagged round the defenders as if he was weaving between his mats. And he did that quick little tip-tap shuffle he did around his chair. He leaned this way, that way – his arms wide like his poster of Ryan Giggs. No one knew which way the little trickster would dodge next.

Tom's dad cheered proudly.

The boys were amazed.

And Mr Bunn just stared at the new star striker he'd picked for the team.

But when Tom looked up he saw something he *never, ever* saw in his bedroom! A big, fat defender, running at

him like a wild hippo! Tom slowed up, not sure what to do. Too late! The wild hippo crashed into him! Tom gasped. Studs scraped down his leg. "Ooh!" A knee sunk into his stomach. "Oof!" An elbow pushed his nose in and made him cry. "Aah-ah!"

"STOP THE GAME!" his mother screamed as Tom fell down into the mud and the defender dribbled away.

Tom stood up, all by himself in the centre circle. He couldn't get his breath back and his whole body was bruised and painful. The game had moved right back to their own penalty area. And when the ball was booted over his head towards *their* goal again he was the only one up there . . . him and the big defender!

"Go on, Tom! Go for it!" the others yelled.

"Hurry!" Mr Bunn instructed.

"Quick, Tom! Go!" his dad shouted.

But Tom had had enough. Maybe he *was* too small. Maybe everyone was right. He just stood there and let the wild hippo get the ball.

Mr Bunn groaned.

His dad looked down.

The boys stopped shouting.

The fat boy was going to boot the ball right back up again . . . but, for some reason, Tom got mad and ran at him! "YOU WAIT, ELEPHANT-BUM!" he yelled. "I'M TOUGHER THAN I LOOK!" He zipped across the wet grass like David Beckham and bashed into him. Heads cracked together. Knees bruised thighs. Boots hammered ankles. But it didn't hurt when *Tom* was doing it to *him*! The ball bobbled free and he wriggled away with it and raced off towards the goal.

The goalie came out. Tom swerved left, then right . . . leaned over . . . swung his foot in a perfect arc . . . and *whacked* the ball with all his anger!

The goalie dived . . . stretched . . . grabbed . . . but it flew past his fingertips . . . a perfect, curving banana-shot . . . right into the top corner of the net!

"GO-O-O-AL!" the whole world roared!

Tom rose on the shock of sound and punched the air. The team were on him, swinging him around and slapping his back. His face was mud-scarred and red. His hair was plastered down flat. And his legs were streaked with rabbit-poo stains.

"He looks *different*!" his mother said.

"Yeah. Sort of *older*!" his dad agreed.

The crowd cheered as Tom had the ball
again, dribbling and dodging and jinking
around the other team.

"Look at him!" they said.

"He's speedy!"

"And tricky!"

"And a super shooter!"

Full-time score . . . two-one to them!

* * *

The Lord Mayor presented Briggsy with a massive silver cup! And Mr Bunn hung a gold medal round Tom's neck. His mother went to pat him on the head but pulled her hand away. He laughed and looked around at his new world.

Streetlights were coming on. And shadows were gathering under the hedge on the far side of the field . . . shadows . . . which seemed to be moving! *Walking*! They weren't shadows! They were . . . *werewolves*! Two of them! Creeping along, hand-in-hand, with masses of . . . *shopping*! Curtain material . . . chairs . . .

and tomato plants! *IT WAS WOLFIE! AND TARA!* They stopped by a gap in the hedge . . . *and kissed! "Oh, Wolfie!"* Then they ducked through the hedge . . . into the forest . . . and were gone.

"Come on, Tom!" the boys yelled at him. "We're gonna play footie against the wall!"

"Oh, no, Albert!" his mother protested." We can't let him run around in the dark!"

"He'll be all right, dear," his dad told her. "The school lights are on, anyway."

So Tom ran over to the playground. He was cold, wet, muddy and sweaty. His nose was running and his whole body tingled with bruises. But he was happy . . . and laughing . . . and charging around after the ball . . . just like everyone else!

THE END

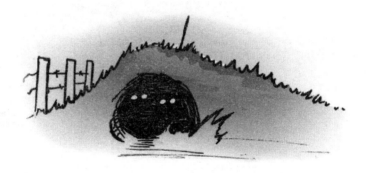